The Other Side of the Bridge

A Story of Racism, Redemption, and Reconciliation

Timothy E Paul

Dorrance Publishing Co
585 Alpha Drive
Pittsburgh, PA 15238
Visit our website at *www.dorrancebookstore.com*

ISBN: 979-8-8860-4208-5
eISBN: 979-8-8860-4861-2

The Other Side of the Bridge

A Story of Racism, Redemption, and Reconciliation

Foreword

Caution! If you are easily offended, you may not get past the second page, but try, for you will be rewarded. Racism comes in all colors, as does good and evil.

The 30th Anniversary Selma March finds two black clergymen with opposing ideologies being the targets for murder. The book is FICTION. All characters are fictitious, except for an ex-president and a celebrity. All the locations are real. The grammar spoken then, and some instances now, reflect that of the local populace.

For most readers, this story will not have the usual slant.

Enjoy,
Timothy E. Paul

Chapter 1

Tee rattled his jail cell door.

"Hey, Big Nig, turn that rap crap off and bring me my pills."

"Look man, get back from the door. I got yo medicine right here. By the way, it's Big Ned. You can call my music crap, but you call me 'Big Nig' again, and you ain't getting no supper. You gonna fry on the inside or the outside. Either way, the bad man is coming for you. You dumb honky, don't you know you can't kill a black man these days?" Big Ned smirked. "I know you gonna be excited, yo new lawyer is waiting to speak to you, but dere ain't no lawyer helping you out of this one. You ain't going nowhere."

Tee shouted at the one-time bar bouncer as he walked away from the cell:

"Hey! How about something to drink, like a Co cola? How about some peanuts? What about prison reform? I got my rights too, or is that just for the bros?"

A woman strolled down the corridor towards the cell.

"Oh, hell! Is this a sick joke?" Tee murmured.

"Mr. Teitel, my name is Miss Jemilla Parks, and I have been designated to represent you." Jemilla Parks was a cross between Aunt Jemima and Oprah. All Jemilla needed was a head scarf. Big, black and every bit of 260 pounds with a rear end like a plow mule.

She continued, "Mr. Teitel, calm down. We have a lot on our plate and very few sympathizers. You made national news, and one cable network wants to do an interview. You need to lose the 'n' word, or no one will listen to anything you have to say. Sometimes there is a backlash after the initial shock and condemnation in a high-profile murder. You just might win some support in high places with a better attitude."

Tee's bright blue eyes flashed.

"Daz right, Oprah. I don't really care about making friends, but I will be remembered for getting rid of that loud mouthed nigger."

"Mr. Teitel, I did not ask to represent you. The state of Alabama has appointed me as your counsel. You could have had a high-powered attorney, but you're too cheap. Now, if you can refrain from the racial slurs, we will get started."

"Okay, darky."

Jemilla countered, "Okay, Jew boy. Tell me what happened."

"I have cancer. My doctors say I have less than a year to live. So, why not kill the SOB? The world would be a better place without him. I figured I might be caught, but I got nothing to lose. As you know, the wheels of justice turn real slow."

"So, you did kill the Reverend?"

"I ain't sure, I think I missed."

"Now, Mr. Teitel, did you not fire a shot from a window overlooking the march?"

"Yes, I did, but I think I may have missed. Someone may have beaten me to the punch, but I would like to get credit for the kill. I would consider it a real trophy. He could go in my study next to my other mounts."

Tee was going to be remembered as the next James Earl Ray, either a hero or a villain.

"You know they found guns all over your place. Seriously, Mr. Teitel, you must tell me the complete truth. I need the whole story if I'm going to represent you.

Chapter 2

A BLOCK OFF BROAD STREET, THE DOWNTOWNER Café was packed. People of all persuasions love good food, and this place was famous for down-home cooking and always consistent, never a bad meal. People passing through Selma went out of their way to stop and eat at the Downtowner. Not much on ambiance, but the fresh vegetables and homemade pies were legendary.

On this particular day, police officers Twitty and Byrd were chowing down with some old high school friends who frequently got together to catch up on one another. Candied yams, crowder peas, fried green tomatoes, turkey and dressing, and collards were washed down with sweet tea.

Day Day Trussel opted for a bacon cheeseburger. Day Day had always struggled with his weight but had managed to be a popular sort. He oozed southern charm, had a heavy accent, and was always attired in a Seersucker sport coat, no matter what the season.

The women in the café had their eyes trained on Officer Byrd. Tall, dark-haired, blue-eyed, and handsome, he was a real ladies' man. He had been a star athlete in school.

Suddenly, all eyes and ears in the café were glued to the small television near the cash register. President Clinton was delivering a message on racial harmony in advance of the upcoming event in Selma, the thirtieth anniversary of the famous 1965 Selma to Montgomery march. Junior commented on his disdain for the liberal SOB, and most local whites felt the same way.

Tee entered the café and pulled up a chair at Twitty's table.

"What's happening, Tee?"

"Don't know it, how about you? I think I'm going to the beach for a few days. The doctors say to enjoy the time I have left. I'll probably go to my cousin's cabin in Panama City. Oysters are still in season, and the cobia are just starting to bite," Tee replied.

"Eat some for me," Junior chuckled.

"Gonna be back for the march, ain't you?" said Jimbo.

"I think one march in a lifetime is enough. Y'all enjoy it, I'll catch it on the tube," replied Tee.

Tee used the men's room at the rear of the café, slipped out the back door, and pulled away in his late father's old Mercedes station wagon.

Twitty, usually the comedian of the group, asked his friends if they noticed how much Tee's cancer had caused him to age.

"I dunno," said Junior. "Tee may beat this; he's got some great doctors up at UAB."

The group finished up, paid their checks, and left the Downtowner. Byrd and Twitty walked together toward their patrol cars.

"Twit, are we still on for tomorrow night?"

"You bet," replied Twitty.

Chapter 3

TEE PARKED THE MERCEDES IN THE CITY LOT BEHIND his dad's old store. It was 2:00 A.M., and the town had rolled up and gone to bed. This would be his trial run. Under complete darkness, he opened the door to the store. His dad had been a super merchant. Jewish by birth, he had natural merchandising skills that he honed from his father's department store, closed for many years now.

Tee used his lock picking skills that he learned from his older brother. He trained Tee well. The door opened on the first try.

The store was pitch black and smelled of must and mothballs with a hint of dust. He groped his way towards the stairwell and bumped into an old clothing rack. His rifle barrel struck the metal frame, making considerable noise. He would avoid making that mistake in the future. Away from the door, he switched on his headlamp. As he walked past the old elevator, memories surfaced of his dad letting him work as the elevator operator. He would deliver customers to their chosen floors. As he climbed the stairs, he mentally recalled the order.

"First stop, Mezzanine. All out. Second floor, Millinery, Ready to Wear, and Accounts Receivable, watch your step," Tee would announce in his 10-year-old voice. Customers thought he was adorable. Well, times had changed. Now in his forties, he was just a sick man, looking every bit of 65 years old.

About 25 more steps, and he found the old display window. It had been replaced years ago, but the platform with the manne-quin was still there. He opened the rear door and light from the street below gave some illumination. He cut his headlamp and climbed onto the platform. Outside, the town was empty, except for the occasional vehicle moving down Broad Street. Tee, only 5'9", would still fit in the box, but the platform creaked under his 185 pounds.

It should hold me, he thought.

He remembered the first day of the original march in 1965. As a 15-year-old, he sat in the display window and watched the daily procession of marchers who were stopped short of crossing the Edmund Pettus Bridge, located one and a half blocks from his perch. The crowd was mostly black folks, with a sprinkling of hippie types and college kids in the mix, singing protest songs and chanting slogans. Since that time, Tee had watched his town regress into a bankrupt, crime infested battlefield, with little fu-ture in sight. Selma had lost 30 percent or more of its population, lost its thriving Air Force Base, and was considered a bad place to conduct business; an even worse place to rear children. As a result, Tee had lost his real estate business and then his family.

Tee would soon exact justice. Reverend Dalton would be an easy target, a small frame with an oversized head. At about 60 to 70 yards, and with a muzzle velocity of 2850 feet per second, the hollow-point would make a mess of his face. There would be virtually no recoil. Dalton would fold on the spot with no chance of survival. Tee's buddy on the police security detail said that at some point in the march, Dalton would be at the intersection of Selma Avenue and Broad Street.

ENOUGH! He climbed off the platform and placed his Remington 243 rifle, a box of 95 grain hollow-point cartridges, and his binoculars on the carpet for his return. He replaced the old half torso mannequin back on the platform. When he returned, he would be fully prepared. It was 2:45 A.M. Tee slipped out the door and into the parking lot. He drove his dad's old car to his house and parked in the garage. He turned out all lights that could be seen from the street. He was in bed within 20 minutes but was restless with anticipation of what was to come. He would now hunker down; he was good to go!

Chapter 4

THE REVEREND MICAH WILLIAMS WAS A GOOD MAN. He was also quite handsome, standing at 6'2" with some graying at the temples. "Born again and washed in the blood," he joined the movement to bring peace and change, but without malice. Change would have to come from the heart. Never violence. Progress was not progress if taken by force. Forgiveness, not vengeance, was his often-used phrase.

Micah had legions of supporters, both black and white. He was humble, soft-spoken, and non-threatening. And it was for this reason, the media hated him. His critics called him an "Uncle Tom." They needed conflict and chaos. They knew their audience and ratings would soar if riots and looting ensued, even higher if violence and blood were shed. After all, Micah Williams wasn't black enough.

But they had their man: the Reverend Pal Dalton. Dalton had many run-ins with the law and was famous for "shaking down" large corporations "for the good of the civil rights movement." He had his own TV show and was considered by many to be their voice. Dalton would be in Selma to stir it up under the disguise of his religious façade. He was like an arsonist, stoking the flames of hate. Loud and rhythmic in tone, Dalton could captivate those of poor judgement, of which there were many. Cynicism and sarcasm ruled his tirades. The media both loved and feared him. Both pastors were expected at the event.

Five days before the march, Reverend Williams spoke to a crowd of about 600, mostly black, on the steps of Brown Chapel. The church had been made famous by the oratories delivered by the late Dr. Martin Luther King during the original 1965 march.

He began his sermon on forgiveness and the Lord's Prayer. The emphasis was on the word "as," noting that we pray for forgiveness AS we forgive those who trespass against us. He further stated that if God is to freely forgive us, we must freely forgive others. Many "Amens" erupted from the throng.

Suddenly, shots rang out, sending the multitude in a stampede in all directions. Sonny, the town terrorist, was hiding behind the chapel. He was a troubled youth and prankster. He loaded his sling shot with cherry bombs, pulled the sling back until the fuse of the explosives touched his lit cigarette dangling from his lips, and launched several cherry bombs into and above the crowd. Many worshippers fell onto the street; others began to call on the Lord for help.

When the police arrived, an officer with a bullhorn announced that there was no attack, but rather a sick prank perpetrated by a bystander. The blasts were merely fireworks, and the chapel area was now secure. Meanwhile, Sonny had gathered up his remaining fireworks and slipped away into the adjoining housing project.

Within 15 minutes, the crowd had re-assembled, and Reverend Williams continued his message. It was one of non-violence, Bible-based, and truth. The crowd reacted to his sincerity with, "Yes, Lord, Yes," and thunderous applause.

Chapter 5

THE NEXT MORNING, TEE TURNED ON THE TELEVISION, and two prominent clergymen were debating race relations and the progress of the civil rights movement. One was white, the other black. The discussion was heated, and fireworks ensued. Tee credited the moderator for trying to stop the clergymen from talking over one another.

"Why are there so many more people of color in prison than white folks? I'll tell you why, indiscriminate racial profiling, that's why!" exploded the black clergyman.

The white clergyman responded, "Why are so many more people of color committing violent crimes?"

"Because they have no food, they must loot and rob 'the haves' to live!"

"They have no food because they will not work, and they steal to buy and sell drugs."

"Why must I experience fear when a patrol car is in my rear-view mirror?" asked the black clergyman.

"Why are whites afraid to even drive through certain parts of town?" was the counter response.

The debate raged on. After an hour of this debacle, there was a handshake and a somewhat cordial parting of the two. However, little progress was identified, no great revelations, and lastly, no clear winner. Both clergymen dug in their heels and asserted their stance, clear that they must be the victor.

Tee knew which side was correct, and he would soon make things right. He changed the channel. The national news gave a less than objective and far left slant. Nothing new.

In disgust, he switched channels again but could find no solace. Different network, but the same tired old slant. His hate for the media on a scale of 1 to 10 was now a solid 11.

"I'll give that sorry lot something to blab about," he said to the TV.

Television was idiocy except for sports and documentaries. Nothing to watch now. No *Little Rascals*, no *Honeymooners*, and certainly no *Amos 'n Andy*.

Switching to his VCR, he found peace in the voice of Keith Jackson.

"Lamar Thomas is on the way down the sideline. GEORGE TEAGUE RUNS HIM DOWN...HE TAKES THE BALL AWAY FROM HIM. TEAGUE HAS GOT THE BALL!"

Tee watched the play two more times. Now he had some sense of calm. It was Tee's favorite play from his favorite game. Alabama vs. Miami for the 1992 national title in the Sugar Bowl. He knew the player's names and idolized the legendary coach Bear Bryant from earlier years. College football to Tee was a haven when the rest of the world was sheer madness. In some weird way, maybe Alabama football would soothe him, a balm for his soul.

He watched several football game replays over the next few days. When he tired of football, he would content himself with oldies music from the sixties.

Tee would not leave his home again until the day of the march. Tee was not going to the beach.

Chapter 6

Ninety miles north of the bridge, the Reverend Pal Dalton stepped off the plane in Birmingham with an accompanying entourage of four. Three black men and one white man, all built like NFL players, attired in black suits, packing heat and remote communications. One might assume they were well paid. Destination: Selma; just two hours away in a black limo.

Dalton hoped his media buddies would be awaiting his arrival.

Dalton's black limo cruised down Broad Street. The scene in Selma was not what he had hoped for. Apparently, no one was aware of his arrival. There were no visible signs along his route, just another tired southern town.

With the march just four days away, there was no indication that anything out-of-the-ordinary was occurring. Obviously, Micah Williams was stealing his thunder. *Why would anyone listen to that Uncle Tom?* thought Dalton. *He has no call for action; no fire in his belly.*

A strategy formed in Dalton's head.

"I can do something about Micah Williams," he said under his breath.

The limo turned onto Water Avenue at the foot of the bridge and stopped one block away at the St. James Hotel. The hotel was situated on a high bluff overlooking the Alabama River and the famous Edmund Pettus Bridge. Some rooms had a view of the bridge. The old hotel was originally built in 1836 and had recently been renovated, replete with the old southern charm. Old brick and New Orleans style French Quarter black wrought iron trim greeted the guests. The hotel often served as a venue for wedding receptions, class reunions, and other social events. He made the hotel his headquarters.

Dalton checked in and was given the top suite. Likewise, his entourage were given adjoining rooms opening out to the center courtyard.

Once settled in, Dalton began to formulate a plan. The apparent lack of interest in him and his agenda stirred Dalton's ire. He must somehow eliminate the competition and draw attention to himself and his message. The country needed a jolt. One way or another, he would have the nation focus on himself.

The next day, Dalton held a rally with the bridge as a backdrop. He was greeted with about 75 followers. Two reporters and a TV crew with CNN were present. He spoke for about 15 minutes and fielded a few questions.

Back at the hotel, he held a meeting with his entourage and made a couple of telephone calls. He had a solid plan, he thought, and he would set it in motion before his confidence waned.

Chapter 7

U~NDER THE BRIDGE AT~ 1:45 A.M., A 13-FOOT B~OSTON~ Whaler eased out from the ramp. It was dark, although there was enough moonlight to navigate without running lights. It was imperative that the cover of darkness conceal their coming nefarious activities.

The 40-horse Mercury and the river's current were more than sufficient for the two occupants. Destination: Blackwell's Bend, a locally famous sandbar just a few miles downstream. In the summer, the Bend, also known as "Little Miami," was a destination for local boaters. Waterskiing, sunbathing, and partying were the typical summer activities.

The place would be desolate tonight. Officers Twitty and Byrd beached the small boat.

From the woods above the sand, two hooded silhouettes approached the men. The four converged, and an exchange was made. No words were uttered. An uncomfortable amount of light reflected off the sand. Byrd noticed one of the two had a tooth, either gold or silver, that shone in the moonlight. Other than the tooth, there were no other distinguishable features. The two parties returned by their same paths. Byrd and Twitty embarked in the Whaler, placing a large black satchel into the boat, while the two strangers returned to the woods.

The return upstream was uneventful. The Whaler skimmed across the smooth black waters, even with the extra cargo of $300,000. The glow from the town's lights shone ahead. Within minutes, the officers passed under the bridge. Once ashore, they confirmed the amount of cash and found themselves with visions of newfound wealth dancing in their heads, alongside fears of being caught.

"What if someone saw us? What if the two strangers were FBI, and this was a set up?"

"Knock it off, Twit! You're making me paranoid."

The "what if's" would haunt the officers for the next two days. But, for the moment, greed would override their anxieties.

The two strangers had similar apprehensions, but they were professionals. They knew stress was part of the job. When they reached their pickup truck, they checked to see if the small papers were still pinched in place by the closed-door seals. No new tracks around the vehicle; primitive security was better than nothing. They made the short drive back to Selma, with one quick stop by the post office drop box. They continued to the St. James Hotel.

Chapter 8

At 3:20 a.m., there was a knock on Dalton's door. The two men shuffled into his quarters.

"Did the meeting go without a hitch?" Dalton asked.

"Yes, no one around, and the officers were on time."

Dalton smiled.

"Good job, gentlemen. Let's celebrate!"

They went next door to another team member's room. Shots were already lined up on the countertop.

"Here's to the 'movement,'" Dalton robustly said.

"To the movement," they replied.

"Bottoms up. Here's to Selma!"

One of the two said, "Sir, we would like to collect our funds and be on the road."

"Sure," replied Dalton, "wait here, and I'll go to my room and get the proceeds." Before Dalton could return, the two slumped to the floor, dead on the spot.

Dalton had two of his group load them up. The bodies would be disposed according to the plan he and his entourage had devised. One man would be the lookout while the others drug the bodies out the side entrance. The bodies were then thrown unceremoniously into the bed of an old Ford pickup truck rented from an elderly black man in east Selma.

Two of the entourage pulled away from the hotel. The drive would take about 20 to 25 minutes to an old ghost town at the confluence of the Alabama and Cahaba Rivers. Cahaba happened to be the first permanent capital of Alabama, but after a few years of flooding, the capital was forced to be moved to its present location in Montgomery.

Once a prosperous town with a booming trade along the Alabama River and down to Mobile, Cahaba's fate was sealed by the catastrophic floods. The area still bore some scars of earlier days. Mostly graveyards, standing chimneys, and a few ramshackle houses.

Many of the homes of the wealthy were consumed by fire many years ago. Some streets of clay remained and talk of restoring the old town surfaced every few years.

Nooses were placed around the necks of the soon-to-be infamous corpses. The ropes were thrown over the 12-foot-high limb of a huge oak tree along the Alabama River. The bodies were doused with gasoline. The center section of the ropes were wrapped around the trailer hitch, so as the truck pulled slowly away, the dead men rose. The ends of the rope were then tied to the large tree trunk. The men eased the truck forward, pulled the cotter pin from the hitch, and watched as the bodies jerked and the dead men swung into their final position. They retrieved the truck-owner's hitch and replaced it on the vehicle.

One of the team struck a match and lit the gasoline-soaked bodies. The other man grabbed a cross made of wood and rags from the rear of the truck, also drenched with gas. The cross was placed just in front of the swingers and lit. The two men cranked up with just one remaining task to perform.

In Selma, Buddy Dence's phone rang, jostling him from sleep. Sluggishly, he rolled over and answered it.

"You got two niggers hanging from a tree out here at Cahaba."

"Who is this?" Buddy shouted.

Click! The line went dead. The hitman hurled his flip phone into the muddy waters of the Alabama River.

"Let's go!" They sped away with the flaming bodies in their rear-view mirror.

Buddy, a reporter for the local paper, *The Times*, noted it was 4:30 A.M. Coffee could wait. He threw on his jeans and grabbed his camera and ran out the door. He would make the drive to Cahaba in just 20 minutes. As he neared the river, he could see the bodies ablaze and a burning cross below them. He snapped dozens of pictures of the two bodies now silhouetted against first light. Visions of a Pulitzer and a big promotion loomed in front of him.

Nationally acclaimed, he thought. *I won't be a short, unnoticed, part-time reporter anymore.*

Buddy stopped and called the sheriff's department, who subsequently sent a patrol car out to the scene. Buddy had an exclusive that would be national news.

Huge, he thought. He was correct.

The two accomplices drove to a house in East Selma to return the borrowed truck to its rightful owner. The elderly black man was thrilled to receive $200 for the very "short-term rental." They added another $50 for cleaning the smell of gasoline from the vehicle. The old man gave them a ride back to the St. James Hotel.

"Mission accomplished," they reported to Reverend Dalton.

The corpses were transported to the morgue. Officers Byrd and Twitty heard news of the hangings and decided to look at the bodies. After a brief viewing of the charred remains, Byrd and Twitty climbed into their patrol car. Both concluded the two victims were the same two individuals who delivered the stash to them at Blackwell's Bend. Byrd immediately noticed the gold tooth that he observed the night of the exchange, and his anxiety mounted.

"Hey, Twitt, do you think we might get murdered or targeted?"

"Byrd, I think we screwed up. We are in over our heads. These people play for keeps. We need help."

After more discussion, the two decided to bury the stash in Old Live Oak Cemetery. Twitty stopped by his house to grab a shovel. They located a gravesite that had been recently filled. No headstone yet; the dirt was still soft. Perfect. At 12:30 A.M., patrol cars in cemeteries are never questioned; after all, they were the good guys. Within 15 minutes, the deed was done. They noted the location of the deceased's grave to prevent disorientation later. The following day, they discovered the deceased was Catherine "Cat" Berger.

"Hey Byrd, Old Cat Berger died a rich woman and didn't even know it!" Twitty said. They both forced a laugh.

Chapter 9

A BIG SMILE ERUPTED ON DALTON'S FACE AS HE watched the news. Apparently, some racist rednecks had murdered two harmless black men, hanging them and setting them on fire. The pictures Buddy Dence had taken flashed on the screen.

The commentator implied that this evil deed must have been the work of a right-wing racist group, most likely the Klan.

The U.S. attorney general guaranteed that justice would prevail.

"Please stay calm," he added. "The perpetrators will be apprehended and prosecuted to the fullest extent of the law. This is a despicable act against black people, a heinous human rights violation."

Dalton's phone rang. CNN and NBC wanted a comment. Dalton arranged another press conference at the foot of the bridge. He made it clear he would not field any questions but would deliver a statement.

That morning, Dalton appeared on every major network.

Tee watched the news of the Cahaba tragedy and was torn between elation and grief. *Two more of them gone*, he thought, yet he felt remorse. These guys had families and friends. Indeed, the world was going to hell. He chastised himself for being too soft.

The channel shifted to a live picture of the Reverend Pal Dalton with the Pettus Bridge as a backdrop. He began to rail.

"No justice, no peace, the movement will not cease! We will bring this town to its knees, if necessary. We will not return to the Jim Crow era! We will fight! We will burn! We will do whatever it takes! These two men were guilty of no crime. They had their whole lives in front of them. Who will care for their families? We will not stop our civil unrest until we have satisfaction. This was not an isolated event by some racist thugs. ALL conservatives share the blame."

He had the cadence and rhythm that his listeners adored. He would, of course, pause and gaze to the side for dramatic effect. The reverend continued for 20 more minutes, stirring the listeners' most primal instincts. Dalton was a master of playing the race angle.

"Where were the police? Where is the governor? The government must do more!"

The politicians and celebrities saw huge opportunities as Dalton's words triggered their raw emotions. The celebs, the media, and the politicians were now headed for Selma to capitalize on the recent racist tragedy.

Three blocks from the bridge, Police Chief Tommy Maas had been watching the national news from his office. He felt the reverend had less than genuine remorse. His secure phone chimed.

"Chief, this is Governor Wimple." The governor of the great and sovereign state of Alabama had been monitoring the news from three hours away in his beach-front condo near Gulf Shores, Alabama. Reluctant to get involved, he decided to extend his vacation with his family. After all, it was spring break. His aides pleaded with him to issue a statement.

Chief Maas replied with sarcasm, "Hey Governor, How's the beach?"

Now angered, the governor demanded, "I want to know, who is in control around there?"

"I need some help, Governor," the chief replied.

"How about 100 National Guardsmen?" the governor offered.

"Not enough," replied the chief.

"Okay, I'll call Colonel Hegedorn and try to get at least 200. We are being portrayed as not providing enough security. Any leads on the Cahaba hangings?"

Maas replied, "Nothing yet, but we're working on it."

The governor now knew that he could no longer hide from Selma. He would prepare a statement, calling for unity and a plea for calm.

"Whoever these criminals are that hung the two martyrs will be brought to justice," he wrote as part of his statement and planned TV interview.

Preparations began immediately for the governor to return to Montgomery to try and quell this volatile situation. He had to get it under control. One bad decision could end his Senate aspirations, or his entire political career. He would have to tread carefully.

That evening, riots erupted in Detroit, Baltimore, and Chicago. Stores were looted and several fires set.

President Clinton pre-empted all television with a statement: "Law and order must prevail." The message from the president was clear.

Chief Tommy Maas was the lone white man in the City of Selma government. Trusted and respected by all races, he was fair and just with no double standards regarding the law. His 6'1", 210 pound physique was as imposing as his character, but his dry sense of humor made him approachable. He was perplexed this evening with the whole march situation.

He answered an unexpected knock on the door, "Come in."

"Chief, may we have a word with you?"

"Sure."

Silently, two officers entered and sat, hesitated for an uncomfortable minute, then Twitty spoke.

"Sir, can this conversation be confidential?"

"Yes, what's up?"

Byrd spoke first and told the Chief about the phone call he had received. The voice sounded familiar but was muffled, revealing the details of the plot to assassinate Micah Williams. He disclosed that the two men they had met were the latter two charred martyrs at Blackwell's Bend, and that they had received cash—$300,000—all in $100 bills.

"We're not 100 percent sure Dalton supplied the cash, but it sure smells like it. Our instructions were to disappear at a certain moment during the march."

Both men were uncomfortable, tearing up.

"As you know, Chief, we are the primary escorts for Micah Williams."

"I need more details," responded Chief Maas.

"Two blocks from the bridge, we would hear a certain signal. At that point, we would fall away into the crowd."

"What would be the signal?"

"A Bobwhite whistle."

"A Bobwhite whistle?"

"Yes, you know, a quail mating call." Byrd demonstrated a Bobwhite call. "Upon hearing the signal, we would move away from Micah Williams."

"Then how was he to be assassinated?"

"We don't know. That info was not given to us. We assume it might be a pistol with a silencer. Please forgive us, Chief. We are trying to do the right thing. We realize we made a horrible error in judgement."

Maas cradled his head in his hands, running his fingers through his crew cut, listening in total shock and disbelief. Looking down at his desk, he paused and didn't speak for a few minutes. There was total silence.

Chief Maas looked up and said, "Look guys, I think we can thwart the assassination and get to the bottom of its origins. If we are successful, I will go to bat for you because you came forward, but I can't make any promises."

The three men stood, and Chief Maas prayed with them.

The two officers turned to leave but were stopped by the chief.

"Hey, men, where's the stash?"

"Buried in Old Live Oak Cemetery," Byrd replied.

"Alright. Meet me here at 12:00 A.M., and we will retrieve the money together. Bring a shovel," he added.

"Yes sir," they replied.

When the two humiliated officers departed, a peace settled over both men as if confession was the first step toward redemption. It was certainly good for the soul.

Chief Maas sat back in his chair and began to devise a plan to protect Reverend Williams and to catch the perps. The three men met that night and drove to the cemetery. After a few tense moments of poor recollection, the officers located the grave. A short dig later, the black case appeared. Twitty stood watch as the Chief took the brief case and placed it on the back seat of the patrol car. The chief confirmed the amount, $300,000, all in $100's.

Upon arrival back at the station, Chief Maas said, "We will all meet with Micah Williams in total privacy. Got it?"

"Yes sir. Look, Chief, we know we screwed up," confessed Twitty.

"Give us a chance to make it right again," they pleaded.

"I believe we can clear you two, protect Reverend Williams, and we bring down the wolf in sheep's clothing, too," replied the Chief.

Byrd turned to the Chief and asked, "What do we do about the money?"

…

No reply.

The two officers turned and left the office.

Chief Maas began to meditate on this dilemma. Someone under his command had been a traitor. Only a select few knew of the planned security, but somebody had betrayed the mission. The enemy had gotten to Byrd and Twitty. The plan had been compromised, or had it?

The chief must consider all angles and options.

Chapter 10

Officer Kirkpatrick was walking and working his beat along Broad Street when someone tapped him on the shoulder.

"Do you know where I can buy a soda pop?" questioned a tall stranger.

"Where are you from?" replied Officer Kirkpatrick.

"Uh, a small town near Birmingham."

"Okay, sure, one block towards the bridge and one block down to the right there's a drugstore."

"Okay. Thank you, sir."

Kirkpatrick noted the sudden change of accent and the term "soda pop." The man proceeded as instructed. The officer also noticed a scar below the man's left eye. He made a mental note. *Hmmm, soda pop, Birmingham, Alabama, accent...it doesn't add up.*

Kirkpatrick didn't much care for Northerners and still referred to them as Yankees. At least this Yankee wasn't wearing socks with sandals.

Nonetheless, the man had committed no crime, so the curious officer continued his beat, proceeding all the way to the bridge. He noticed the same guy crossing in front of the bridge on Water Avenue. Kirkpatrick picked up his pace and spotted the man entering the St. James Hotel.

Kirkpatrick hung around a while, then went back to the station. He conferred with the chief, then drove to within a block east of the St. James Hotel and parked on the opposite side of the street in an unmarked car. There was no activity for some time, until he noticed people gathering at the old train depot, closed now for over 40 years. Twenty or so folks, all white.

Kirkpatrick grabbed his binoculars and took a closer look. Departing the hotel was a large black fellow with a bag of some sort. He proceeded to the depot and appeared to be speaking to the group of whites in congregate. Twenty minutes later, they formed a line; he gave each of them an envelope and turned and walked back to the St. James Hotel as the crowd dispersed in different directions.

Kirkpatrick stayed a while longer, observing no other activities in the area.

The officer drove back to the station and briefed Chief Maas. Kirkpatrick's curiosity was piqued. His gut told him something was not right.

Later that afternoon, a procession of about 20 buses crossed the bridge into downtown. They turned left three blocks later onto Dallas Avenue and back west nearly two miles to a field adjacent to Block Park, the municipal baseball stadium.

The coaches turned left and parked in a line along the wooded creek bank. The New Freedom Riders disembarked with bedrolls, backpacks, and other provisions.

Nearby deputies observed that the Riders consisted mostly of college kids. They were on spring break from schools in Michigan, Illinois, Wisconsin, and Minnesota. Most were 18 to 23 years of age wearing t-Shirts picturing the Pettus Bridge, proclaiming "Make a Difference, Selma '95." They intended to make a difference. These kids were full of idealistic hopes and dreams; perhaps they felt the need for more purpose in their lives. They were called to this "higher mission." They unpacked and set up camp in the large field.

Organizers set up portable bathrooms and water stations at strategic locations.

Overeducated and suffering from poor parenting, this anniversary march would be their moment. That night, there were several small campfires. One large gathering of the Riders was singing old protest songs. Sonny showed up and relieved 10 kids of about $200 on beer chugging wagers. Sonny had perfected the one and a half second "shot-gun" of a 12-ounce beer. No one came close to topping this feat. For an encore, Sonny would have his dog, Gibby, leap up and snatch hot dogs from his mouth. Sonny became very popular with these kids.

The Dallas County sheriff posse stayed at a distance, observing but not interfering. Their instructions were to give them a wide berth and stand down. As the Riders sang Peter, Paul, and Mary's "Blowing in the Wind," there was the distinct smell of pot blowing in the breeze some 200 yards away. The smoke was dense, and the beer was cold. The food vendors were doing a brisk business. The scene took on the flavor of a festival, and good time was had by all. The posse would not react. The morning of the march, the Riders would be bussed to downtown Selma.

Chief Maas called for an emergency meeting of all patrolmen privy to the march security plans. Doors closed, secret and private. Twelve officers were present: Twitty, Byrd, Kirkpatrick, Von Doon, Lack, Causby, Nebro, McCaleb, Peek, Stallworth, Knight, and Parrish. His secretary, Gail, was given permission to leave for the day.

"Listen up. There has been a change in our security plan," said Maas. We are going to change the start time of the march to 9:00 A.M. instead of 10:00 A.M. This will not be made public until the evening before the event, got it? All other details will remain the same."

All replied, "Got it."

That night, Chief Maas met with Byrd and Twitty at the local steak place. The three of them sat in the dark and cavernous bar of the Tally Ho restaurant. Chief Maas informed them there would be no change in the original plan. The meeting they had with all the officers present was to plant disinformation to smoke out the Judas of the group.

After finishing their meal, Byrd and Twitty noticed the chief picked up the tab, paid with cash, and left a sizable tip.

"We will meet with Micah William tomorrow."

At 4:00 A.M., Officer Kirkpatrick took up his position in an old, vacant, three-story building across the street and to the east from the St. James Hotel. From his second-floor window, he had a clear view of the hotel and Water Avenue from the bridge to the old depot. Nothing happened for a few hours of any consequence, except for a few people coming and going in and out of the old hotel.

At about 10:15 A.M., a taxi with a lone passenger pulled up in front of the hotel. The passenger slid out, oddly dressed in unseasonable clothing consisting of a trench coat with the collar turned up.

Kirkpatrick grabbed his binoculars. Officer Von Doon. He was speaking through the passenger side window with the driver.

The taxi remained stationary as Von Doon entered and departed the hotel within 15 minutes. The tall, white stranger with a scar, who would now be known as "Mr. Soda Pop," was by his side. After being handed a manila envelope, Von Doon clutched it to his chest and entered the taxi. The taxi departed the hotel entrance, heading east and disappearing after a left turn before the depot.

Kirkpatrick phoned the chief on his secure line reporting the event. Von Doon had taken the bait.

Chief Maas was not totally surprised. Von Doon had always been a loner, mysterious in a myriad of ways. No one knew exactly where he resided. It was speculated that he lived in a general area in some hills north of town near an old boy's camp.

Von Doon was a competent officer, but rumors about his past were always circulating. His dark complexion, long, black wavy hair, and deep-set eyes gave him a sinister presence. His dad was implicated in the 1960s in the case of three missing campers. The case was investigated, but no charges were ever filed. The case was never resolved, and suspicion remained.

The chief would not confront Von Doon, just yet. He might even be useful.

"Otis?"

"Yessuh?"

"This is Chief Maas. I need to meet with you and the Reverend Williams ASAP."

"Okay, what's up?" Otis was Micah Williams's chief aide and confidante, who had the Reverend Micah's ear.

"Don't be overly alarmed, but we think there might be an attempt on Micah's life."

"Not alarmed? Is this a serious threat?"

"Yes, and well planned."

"I will have the reverend in your office this afternoon."

"Do not speak about this threat to anyone, got it?"

"Yessuh."

Less than an hour later, Otis called Chief Maas to announce he and Reverend Williams would be at the chief's office in about 30 minutes.

Upon arrival, Otis and Micah were escorted in by the chief's secretary, Gail Gideon. They took a seat in front of the chief's large oak desk.

There was little small talk. The chief informed Micah and Otis that officers Byrd and Twitty, who were standing behind Maas, would still escort them during the march, but at some point near the corner of Selma Avenue and Broad Street, the officers would fall away and disappear into the crowd.

"Mr. Williams, I see you look puzzled, so let me say, there will be at least three other officers dressed as marchers who will move in proximity of you. You will not be able to recognize them from the rest of the throng. You will be wearing body armor, so be sure to wear your largest suit. Mr. Williams, let me assure you we will protect you, and we will track this purported attempt on your life to its origins."

Chief Maas continued, "Micah, if you want to call off your participation in the march, we will understand."

"I knew there would be tribulation on account of my faith, but I am ready. My God did not give me a Spirit of Fear! I'm all in."

Otis's eyes were wide with worry, but he understood Micah's position. He also knew the chief had a good heart and supported the reverend's positions on faith and progress.

The five men rose, and Micah asked the chief, Otis, and the officers to pray with him.

After the prayer, the chief escorted them to the door.

"Gentlemen," he said, "Loose lips sink ships. This plan cannot be revealed to anyone."

"Got it," replied Otis.

"I understand," said Micah.

Chapter 11

Business was good. The town was bustling. Lots of people in town meant lots of money in flow. No rooms were available within 100 miles of Selma, and all restaurants were slammed. Local merchants who chose to stay open were doing brisk sales.

It was amazing how fast the modern-day carpetbaggers set up souvenir stands along the sidewalks of Broad Street. T-shirts sporting the image of the bridge and the slogan "Selma 1995" were popular items, and Micah Williams and Pal Dalton bobbleheads were top sellers, along with buttons with "No Justice No Peace" over Pal Dalton's image. Other pins had the photo of Reverend Micah Williams with "No Jesus No Peace" inscribed.

Broad Street had a carnival atmosphere. Television crews were spotted at various corners conducting interviews. Celebrities and politicians were popping up along the streets of Selma. The Downtowner had people lined up 50 feet along the sidewalk, waiting to sample Selma's southern cuisine.

All eyes turned to look at a convoy of National Guard Jeeps and trucks rumbling over the Pettus Bridge, causing a brief lull in the festivities.

The procession moved down Broad Street, turning left onto Dallas Avenue, making its way to the old and vacant Baptist hospital grounds, where encampment would take place.

Two MP units and one support unit began to unload. Their mission was to deter any mischief or civil disobedience without the use of force. Presence and visibility should be enough. However, the Guard was prepared to engage, if necessary, on the day of the march.

As a show of goodwill, the Guard would hand out bottles of drinking water. They would not carry assault rifles on Broad Street, but they would wear sidearms.

Checkpoints at certain street corners would be established. In order to enhance the image of the National Guard, soldiers would not line the sidewalks but would have a large presence at the approaches to the bridge. In all, the guard numbered about 185 men, all of whom resided in Alabama. Most had families and regular jobs. They wanted to get the job done and go home.

Chapter 12

Tee's disbelief turned to despair. His **VCR** ceased to function. He tried everything in his power to repair it with no luck. He would resign himself to watching regular television channels minus football replays, old westerns, and porn. He would repeat his mantra that the world had, indeed, gone to hell and taken his world with it.

Tee could not sleep. In just four short hours, he would make his way to the old store and set up for the kill. His plan was to park six blocks away in the driveway of a friend's vacant house. The house was listed for sale. He would make the walk and enter his dad's former store in less than 20 minutes.

He turned on the tube but found it impossible to watch anything. He was nervous, but nonetheless committed to the deed. The television was mindless background noise.

He almost drifted off when an old Billy Graham crusade popped up on the screen. It seemed like Graham was speaking directly to him. As a youngster, Tee's mother drug him down to the Presbyterian church most Sundays. He would remember a few things from church, but God was not a reality for Tee. Tee was mesmerized by his words.

Graham said, "Everyone can be forgiven. It isn't about the do's and don'ts. We are incapable of keeping the commandments. Only faith in God's Son will be our ticket."

Humbug, Tee thought. His Jewish dad once told him, "Son, if you don't know Moses, you had better know your noses."

Tee changed the channel. What? It was Micah Williams delivering a sermon on Jesus's two commandments, loving our enemies, forgiveness, and faith. Tee watched intently as Micah Williams continued to speak about salvation. How it is free for anyone who prays, believes, and repents. Tee watched the entirety of the sermon.

Maybe I could change, he thought.

People, places, and events began to flood his mind. He remembered the family housekeeper, Lillian. He loved and missed her so much; she was his main source of being nurtured during childhood. She was often singing, always about her Lord, very low in volume, while ironing the family's clothing. She was always at such peace with herself. He could picture her in the laundry room singing "spirituals."

Tee regretted how his brother and he played juvenile tricks on her—like shaking up a soft drink and placing it in the ice box.

"Lillian!" Tee would yell "Would you fix me a Coke?"

Lillian would waddle to the fridge and take out the bottle and open it. Once open, it spewed all over her, her face dripping with foam.

In times prior, Tee laughed at the memory, but now he felt only shame. He knew he was wrong. He was mean; just plain sorry was what he was then, and now as well.

Tee had another memory come to mind. He and Lillian were standing on the corner near his house, waiting with another family's housekeeper, to ride the bus downtown. Lillian's ride home would pick her up there, and his dad was to meet Tee at the downtown bus stop.

They boarded the bus, shuffled to the back, and sat. Tee was startled when the bus driver bellowed, "Son! You can't sit back there! You must sit here up front!"

It was seven-year-old Tee's first realization that there was a system in place that differentiated between the races.

Weeks later, Tee accompanied his mother as she drove Lillian out to her home in the country. It was the first time Tee had ever seen a house that small, and with a dirt floor.

Tee's mother said Lillian would have to miss work for at least two months. When Tee asked his mother where Lillian was, she just replied, "It is picking season, son. She will be back in a couple of months."

The realization that Tee would be without Lillian made him cry.

More memories raced through his mind. Tee and his late brother Max had committed so many acts of mischief and more. Thirty-five years had passed, and here he was on the verge of committing a terrible crime.

"It has to be done. No, it needs to be done. Dalton must not live," was his justification.

He took a quick shower and prepped himself. Yes, he was nervous but still committed. He fixed himself a thermos of hot, strong coffee and departed for downtown Selma at 2:45 A.M. He parked the Mercedes at his friend's house as planned. He slipped on his camouflage hunting mask and left the automobile.

There was no one visible along the route except one patrol car, parked on the corner of Broad Street and Dallas Avenue. He altered his route and crossed Broad Street on Alabama Avenue. Once across the wide thoroughfare, he continued one block and turned left.

One half block later, he entered the parking lot of his dad's old store. He struggled with the door. He rationalized it was because he was anxious. Eventually, he gained access.

Once inside the building, Tee made the trek through the darkness to the stairwell. Five minutes later, he raised the display window about 18 inches. His rifle, ammo, and binoculars were on the floor right where he had left them. It was 3:10 A.M.

He would leave the half torso mannequin in the display window. He felt certain he would not be noticed. At the appropriate time, he would crawl onto the display window box, and use the window frame to steady his shot.

Got it—all to plan so far, he thought. *Just six and a half hours now, and I'm good to go.*

Tee leaned back and tried to relax, but memories of his estranged wife, Julia, entered his mind. She had been the love of his life; he had not yet found closure with her. Julia had left him due to his drinking and adultery. He had regrets about his behavior. She now lived in Birmingham with their two sons, and he missed them dearly. They might as well be divorced; maybe his cancer would be the solution to that issue, he thought. She would occasionally call a mutual friend and ask about his health. The kids were older now and kept in touch with him, and that was good for Tee's emotional health.

Chapter 13

North of the bridge, some 720 miles—Ohio, to be precise—one Ms. Annie Pearl Jones was worried about her son. She had seen on the news the broadcast of the two black men that were hung. She had not heard from him since he left to meet up with Reverend Dalton's group in Selma, Alabama. That was several days ago.

She called his phone multiple times, but it always went to voicemail. She left numerous messages, but there were no replies. She guessed she might just load up and travel to Selma. In 30 minutes, she was packed.

Backing down the driveway, she stopped to check her mailbox and found a postcard with a picture of the St. James Hotel situated on the Alabama River. She turned it over and the message read:

> *Mama, if you haven't heard from me by the time you receive this card, I fear something bad may have happened. I think Dalton is up to something.*

Annie Pearl's heart sank. She called the number on the post-card for the hotel, asking if her son was registered there.

"No ma'am. Reverend Dalton has several rooms, but we don't have the names of all the occupants."

She thanked the desk clerk, reversed out of the driveway, and set her mind on the mission to find her son, making the drive without an overnight stay.

As she drove, a myriad of thoughts rumbled through her mind. She had never had a good feeling about her son's association with Reverend Dalton. She beat herself up with thoughts of raising her son as a single parent. She rationalized that she did the best she could with the little bit she possessed. Her intentions were good. She forced herself to focus on the drive, keeping her emotions in check.

She was a small woman, her feet barely touching the pedals. However, her stature would not deter her from helping her son. It would be a long night.

Annie Pearl realized she needed as much information as she could obtain before her arrival in Selma. When she stopped for gas and called the Dallas County coroner, her worst fears were confirmed. He could not identify the bodies due to being too badly burned. The bodies were sent to the state forensics lab in Montgomery. But the coroner remembered that one of the two bodies had an identifiable gold bicuspid.

"Oh my God!" was heard, and then a click. Annie Pearl slumped over the steering wheel and wept uncontrollably. Her boy had been murdered, probably by Dalton's bunch.

Her sobs turned to rage. She would take matters into her own hands. Determined, she drove on, stopping only for personal ne-cessities and fuel.

Exhausted, Annie Pearl arrived in Selma at 7:00 A.M. She parked in the only available spot—a handicapped parking place in a church parking lot a block off Broad Street. Getting fined or towed was the least of her concerns. She sat in the vehicle, watching hundreds of college kids tumble from buses and heading to the march.

She reached into the glove box and grabbed her small pistol, sliding it into her purse. She took a deep breath, exited the car, and joined up with the "New Freedom Riders," walking toward the historic Edmund Pettus Bridge.

As the Alabama National Guard began to settle into its encampment, a tall, white stranger was surveying the group. Eventually, he located a tall GI whom he approached and initiated a conversation. After the small talk, the two men went separate ways, but the infiltrator kept an eye on the tall soldier.

Once he determined which tent belonged to the GI, he knocked and entered his quarters.

"Sir, is it possible that I might purchase a uniform from you? This may be a little out of order, but I will pay you $300 for the shirt, pants, and a hat."

"Really?" he replied. "Sure, we were all supposed to pack an extra set. If necessary, I can get another set. The state furnishes them for us, but please don't tell anyone."

"Great, I have always wanted a combat uniform. It will be perfect for my hunting trips. By the way, what is your mission?"

"Well, we will try and keep the peace and hand out water to anyone that is thirsty. We don't want any problems."

"You don't say, what kind of water are you giving out?"

"Bottled water, like the cases stacked by the truck over there."

"Sure, hey, thank you, man!" He collected his purchase and departed into the darkness, headed for the St. James Hotel.

He spotted a nearby convenience store, and purchased a tube of glue, and two bottles of water identical to the bottles the Guard would provide to the marchers

He made his way back to the hotel, opened both bottles, and put a few drops of a substance into the liquid. He took the slightest smear of glue to reseal the caps to the white rings, so it appeared unopened. He placed a very small marker on the top of the caps and placed them in the fridge.

Chapter 14

The day had arrived. At 10:00 a.m., Micah Williams addressed a huge crowd from the steps of Brown Chapel. The message was supposed to be televised nationally. Thousands of folks could not get close enough to see the reverend, so large speakers were set up for a quarter of a mile in two directions.

Williams spoke again about progress through forgiveness. As Christians, the great commission was to evangelize, not terrorize. One cannot legislate the heart. Only Jesus could change the hearts of both sides of the isle. All have sinned and fallen short, he said.

He continued his message for another 20 minutes. He then asked the crowd to pray with him. Hundreds had their hands raised toward heaven.

Micah continued, "Forgive us our sins AS we forgive those who trespass against us. Be with us today, guide us, and protect us, and open the hearts of those who do not know you. Let our light go out into the world and change hearts."

The crowd responded "Amen, and Amen."

It wasn't a Sermon on the Mount, but his words pierced the hearts of many that day. His oratory had the feel and emotion of the late Reverend Martin Luther King.

When finished, the Reverend descended the steps and walked onto the street. His escorts, Byrd and Twitty, moved to his side. Officers Parish, Peek, and Kirkpatrick were nearby, dressed the same as most of the marchers and blending in unnoticed.

Otis was close by.

Chapter 15

THE ALABAMA STATE TROOPERS HAD CLOSED OFF THE far side of the bridge. All through traffic had been rerouted to the bypass around Selma. All other intersecting streets along Broad Street were blocked for one mile, except for Selma Avenue. Highway 80 was a federal highway, and the event must conclude by 2:00 P.M.

Dalton had set up on the slope of the bridge, about 100 feet from its base. From this perch, he could view several blocks of Broad Street. Members of his entourage flanked him on both sides. Two large speakers rested at the bottom of the bridge.

A crowd of about 800 pressed forward for a better glimpse of Reverend Dalton.

On the west side of Broad Street at the intersection of Water Avenue, a gathering of about 20 or so of Dalton's white trash mercenaries were making their presence known. Five dressed as clan members (sheets and hoods); others were draped in Confederate battle flags. Still, others waved the stars and bars. There wasn't a full set of teeth among them.

Dalton looked upon the scene and could not hide a smile. *Perfect, no one plays the card better than I*, he thought.

A cable news company decided to do some interviews and selected the worst looking among the bunch.

"What purpose do you have here during this historic and hallowed event?"

The guy responded with, "This town is our town. We don't need any high-powered nigga causing trouble. Leave us be! Go back from where you're from. You've already knocked us down, so now you want to kick us."

The rowdy bunch began chanting, "Go to hell, Reverend Pal! Go to hell!"

Dalton began his oratory with, "As you can see, there has been no real progress! These thugs would have you back picking cotton and would turn back the hands of time.

"You will soon be riding in the back of the bus," Dalton continued, talking over a chorus of Dixie from the dirt balls gathered at the base of the bridge. A brief scuffle between a Dalton supporter and a white protester ensued. The cameramen positioned themselves at an angle that made the white group appear much larger.

The troopers quickly intervened, and the whites began to disperse westward down Water Avenue. Dalton's rant continued, "No justice, no peace! We demand reparations; we must have satisfaction. We have been under the chains of white rule for hundreds of years. We cannot tolerate the system. There will be change, one way or another."

Dalton went on with his confabulation for another 10 minutes. The reverend never quoted scripture or referred to the

Bible, which he never carried. The crowd of several hundred listened and occasionally responded favorably.

As Dalton descended from the Edmund Pettus Bridge, he walked through his supporters to lead them down Broad Street away to Selma Avenue. His original plan was to join up with Micah Williams at the intersection of Selma Avenue and Broad Street. But he did not expect to see Micah alive. Once the groups merged, with or without Micah Williams, the media would depict the crowd as being all his followers.

Governor Wimple was watching the televised coverage from his office in Montgomery. He was disappointed that a hundred or so thugs had shown up to cause trouble, according to the commentators.

Chief Maas had just informed the governor that at least 6,000 were on hand to hear Micah Williams.

Thus far, there had been no television coverage of Micah Williams.

An overhead live shot from a helicopter revealed that Dalton's group was much smaller than previously intimated.

"I guess they report whatever they want to report," the governor surmised.

Chief Maas also reported that everything was under control… so far.

Chapter 16

Micah proceeded to walk through the crowd to be in the lead position. Byrd and Twitty walked on either side of Micah, with a local pastor and Otis flanking them. They moved en masse down Sylvan Street to Selma Avenue.

Micah held up his hand and halted the assembly, then turned and faced the crowd. In a loud voice, he proclaimed, "Make a joyful noise unto the Lord."

The multitudes started singing "This is the Day." They took their time and enjoyed the moment, clapping as they sang and walked. The group turned right onto Selma Avenue and began the short journey of four blocks to Broad Street.

There was a National Guard vehicle on every corner of each intersection. Up ahead, there was a gathering of people at the Broad Street intersection.

Throngs of mostly young people were moving up Broad Street from Dallas Avenue. Annie Pearl was among them. All four corners had Jeeps and trucks positioned by the National Guard. The trucks were facing away from the streets with soldiers in the backs of the vehicles handing out bottled water. A few soldiers had mingled into the throng, giving water to those in the center of the march.

Reverend Dalton spotted Reverend Williams's group and began to make his way through the group for a planned rendezvous.

A loud Bobwhite whistle was heard. Byrd and Twitty quickly fell back into the crowd. Within seconds, a tall white man dressed as a soldier appeared from nowhere and forced his way through the crowd holding two bottles of water.

Nothing seemed out of the ordinary until Officer Kirkpatrick, in street clothes, noticed the scar on the soldier's face. BINGO! It was him! Part of Dalton's entourage! The soda pop guy! The man who was with Von Doon!

It all processed in a millisecond. The rangy soldier held out the water bottles to Micah and Otis in an apparent good will gesture.

In a split second, Kirkpatrick launched himself across their outstretched arms just as Otis was reaching for the water. Kirkpatrick slapped away the bottles, hit the ground, and shouted, "Don't drink that water!"

The white imposter began to weave through the masses, pushing and shoving his way through, trying to evade Officer Kirkpatrick, who was in hot pursuit, with Lack and Stallworth close behind. Reverend Williams composed himself. Indeed, something bad had happened.

Officer Peek retrieved the poisoned water bottles. Otis's eyes were wide with worry.

Annie Pearl Jones squeezed her way through the crowd to position herself directly behind Pal Dalton.

Kirkpatrick made his second launch of the day when he tackled Mr. Soda Pop directly in front of the Downtowner. Officers Stallworth and Lack, along with Kirkpatrick, subdued Soda Pop, cuffed him to a light post, and radioed for a squad car.

Reverend Dalton connected with Reverend Williams just east of the intersection.

As they shook hands, Micah said, "Surprised to see me here?"

"Uh, good to see you, Mr. Williams."

As the media and TV crews positioned themselves to cover this historic occasion, Annie Pearl grasped the gun within her purse, held it against Dalton's back, and fired her 9 mm pistol. It would be the last thing he ever felt.

Tee was extremely nervous. His heart was pounding. He started to tremble like he experienced during his first deer hunt.

Control yourself. It must be Buck Fever, he thought.

The marchers were coming up Selma Avenue, and the moment of truth was just moments away. He could see a commotion going on in Reverend Williams's procession, but Dalton was in plain view now and approaching Reverend Williams.

Tee's upper torso was resting on the platform, the window was open, his 243 was locked and loaded. Tee dialed his scope to 7x. Below him was a sea of humanity. Collateral damage would be a possibility.

The two clergymen extended their arms to shake hands. He rested the rifle on the window frame, took a deep breath, and slowly let out a little air. He told himself, "Squeeze, don't pull." He began to shake. He fired anyway.

He didn't feel good about the shot, but he could see that he must have hit someone as people were gathering around a body.

Marchers scattered in all directions. Bystanders began to point up at Tee. Tee slid from the box, laid down the rifle, and began his walk down to the first floor.

As he approached the door to the parking lot, he could hear people talking.

Officers Lack and Nebro forced the door open and shined a flashlight directly into Tee's face.

"Hands up!" was the command.

Tee responded, "I am not armed."

He was forced to lay on the floor, cuffed, and led out to a squad car.

Buddy Dence was nearby, taking pictures of the suspected assassin.

Annie Pearl and Tee had both fired within a second of each other.

Bedlam ensued.

"This event is over!" an Alabama state trooper announced with a bullhorn on the corner of Broad Street and Selma Avenue. "I repeat, this event is over! All of you must vacate. This is a crime scene."

Most participants had already fled in a frenzied rush. Annie Pearl disappeared into the fleeing herd of college kids. Most of the marchers turned onto Dallas Avenue one block away, as Broad Street had been blocked earlier for the march.

Annie Pearl followed the stampede onto Dallas Avenue. Most of the horde began to slow to a walk. Many just ahead were climbing aboard the buses. Annie Pearl reached the church parking lot, but her car was gone.

She hesitated for a minute, looking around; her vehicle was definitely missing. She followed some college kids and climbed aboard a bus. The driver did not count or confirm passengers. Getting out of Selma fast was his only concern. The bus pulled away and was out of the city within 15 minutes.

Annie Pearl clutched her purse across her chest and reflected on what she had done. She was scared. Her heart and mind raced. Did she really just kill someone? Most of the riders were on their phones to parents and friends back in the Midwest, some of which had already seen the TV bulletins of the assassination.

Chapter 17

Tee paced nervously in his cell. He worried he was now a murderer. He was concerned he may have hit an in-nocent marcher.

He heard a commotion, got up from his bench, and watched through the bars as Big Ned and Officer Kirkpatrick escorted a tall, white fellow down the corridor. The bedraggled suspect was pushed into a cell across from Tee.

"Get out of that uniform and put on these coveralls," Big Ned bellowed.

Kirkpatrick stopped on his way out.

"Tee, is that you?"

"Yeah man, it's me."

"So, you're the one who was up in your dad's old store?"

"It was me," Tee replied.

"Good luck, Tee," Kirkpatrick said before departing.

"How about a go plate from the Downtowner?" Tee yelled.

"Can't help you, Tee. Hey, Big Ned, get the new guy a 'soda pop,'" Kirkpatrick shouted as the main door shut.

Reverend Dalton was pronounced dead. His body was loaded into an ambulance. A few of the media were allowed to photograph and record the scene.

Within 40 minutes of Dalton's demise, he would once again cross the Edmund Pettus Bridge, this time in silence as his body was being transported to the lab in Montgomery for autopsy.

President Clinton suddenly appeared on all major networks with a plea for calmer heads.

"Justice will be served. The assassin will be captured. He will be held accountable for this reprehensible deed."

That evening, the cable news companies telecast interviews from numerous eyewitness's accounts on the scene in Selma.

One person claimed there were two shots fired. Another claimed there was only one shot, but the echoes from the buildings made it appear as if two shots were fired. Several said it was a conspiracy of sorts. Most of the witnesses said the shot or shots originated from the three-story building about 70 yards away. A third claimed they saw a person in the second-floor window of said building. Another observer said she saw for certain a short black woman holding her purse up to Dalton's back and then heard a gunshot.

The networks had non-stop coverage of the tragedy. Speculation was rampant, and theories were numerous.

The officers in the area believed they heard two shots.

Following the live interviews, a hastily formed round table of "experts" agreed among themselves that "lack of gun control" was the issue.

Senator Schlomo of New York promised to introduce a bill banning all long guns.

Numerous mini documentaries popped up on all major networks. The late reverend was portrayed as a hero, a trailblazer in the civil rights movement. He had modeled his "ministry" after that of Jessie Jackson. A voice of all the people of color, their hope, their warrior, their inspiration! He changed the social consciousness of the nation. His tireless efforts had brought much progress. One of the commentators wept. That night, there was sporadic civil unrest in the form of looting and riots in some major cities across the country.

Chief Maas ordered officers Nebro and Parrish to go to the hotel and search Dalton's rooms. They would not have a search warrant; time was of the essence.

Luckily, the hotel staff accompanied the officers and opened the rooms. The officers found Dalton's room basically undisturbed. They loaded his suitcase, clothing, and all personal effects onto a cart.

When they entered Dalton's associates' rooms, there was a different scene. No suitcases, but clothing, personal belongings, including cash, were scattered all over the floor. It was as if the entourage had made a hasty exit.

One Sig 9 mm pistol and two vials of an unknown substance were collected. They placed that evidence into a bag. They put yellow police tape across the doors, returned to the hotel lobby, and stopped to interview the desk clerk.

She stated three black fellows of Dalton's group had run out of the hotel with a police officer.

"Do you remember when this happened?" asked Parrish.

"I don't remember the exact time, but it was while the march was in progress."

"Can you describe the policeman?" asked Parrish.

"I seen him in here before. Uhh, the other day. He came in for a few minutes, and the tall white fellow from Dalton's group met with him here in the lobby. The officer was white, but dark complected, with kinda wild lookin' eyes."

"Do you remember what time of day that was?" asked Parrish.

"I had the early shift that day, so mid-morning would be my best guess."

"Thank you for that information. We will be back in touch with you later. We need your name and a phone number to contact you for further questions. We have secured the hotel rooms with police tape. We are reminding you that the hotel is now a crime scene, and no one is allowed to enter the rooms. Expert investigators will be by later to take fingerprints and samples, so no one should enter the rooms. That includes guests and employees."

Chapter 18

Chief Maas's secretary knocked then entered.

"Chief, Mr. Martin from Shotgun's Tow and Wrecker is on hold, said he had some interesting info you might want to see."

"Okay, Gail, put him through."

"Hey, Chief, Jimbo here. Listen, we towed a car in yesterday. It has Ohio plates on it, and when we opened the door, an item fell out that you may want to see."

"Really? You know, Mr. Martin, we've had lots of out-of-state people around here this past week."

"I know," replied Martin, "but this isn't a normal situation, right?"

"Right," said the chief.

"Okay, I'll have someone over there shortly."

Chief Maas dispatched Officer Lack over to check it out. He reminded him to follow strict protocol concerning evidence collection.

Forty-five minutes later, Lack called the chief.

"Chief, this could be an important lead."

"Yeah? What is it?"

"It's a postcard from one of Dalton's bunch to the apparent owner of the vehicle."

"I got it. Clean out the glove box, all registration papers, everything. Then have the vehicle towed over here and impounded ASAP. Bring all the contents to my office, got it?"

"Yes sir," Lack responded.

Thirty minutes later, Lack entered the chief's office and plopped the papers on his desk. The owner of the vehicle was Annie Pearl Jones from Ohio. This postcard was a game changer.

Chief dialed the coroner.

"Hey, Randy, Chief here. Have you had any inquiries on the identification of the burned victims?"

"Sure, the usual media type… Well, there was one individual, I believe a woman's voice, that inquired."

"Anything significant in the conversation?" posed the chief.

"Just that she seemed upset when I mentioned that one of the deceased had a gold tooth."

"Thanks, Randy, that's all I needed."

Annie Pearl Jones was now a person of interest. *No*, he thought, *she was a suspect.*

Chief Maas began to review all video footage, and photographs from the last moments of the shooting. There were so many bodies crowded around Reverend Dalton that he could not identify any suspect. Upon further examination of the video, the chief noticed one short black woman mixed into a crowd of mostly young whites, fleeing down Broad Street away from the crime scene.

Chapter 19

CHIEF MAAS had a long night without much sleep. He entered his office, and his secure line rang.

"Chief?"

He responded, "Hello Governor."

"Chief, I just received some information that hasn't been released to the media, so keep this under your hat. Forensics notified me that their preliminary findings reveal the Reverend was shot from behind at point blank range. So, the assassin was not in a building firing down on the target. Furthermore, the two burned victims had traces of cyanide in their bodies. According to the experts, they were dead before they were hung."

"That's very interesting because Gail just gave me the lab report on the water bottles Officer Peek retrieved," Chief Maas replied.

The governor said, "Yes?"

"The water bottles contained cyanide," said Maas. I think it's all coming together now."

"That's very interesting. Thanks for the info. I'm sure we will be talking again soon. I think we are on the right trail," Wimple replied.

Gail knocked and entered, handed the chief an envelope marked "Confidential," and returned to her desk. The envelope contained a letter from Officer Von Doon.

It was short, and simple:

Please accept my resignation effective immediately.

There was no postmark on the envelope. Someone had to have hand-delivered it.

Chief Maas buzzed Gail and asked, "Who dropped off that envelope?"

Gail replied, "The envelope just appeared on my desk while I was at lunch. I don't know… That's strange," she added.

Chapter 20

"CAN YOU BELIEVE IT? TEE'S THE GUY THAT SHOT Dalton!" said Day Day.

His friend Randy replied, "I'm not sure, Trussel. I heard it was a black woman that shot him. I think Tee was at the beach."

"Well, I know Tee is in jail now, that's for sure," responded Day Day.

"Yeah, I'm just glad someone shot the SOB," added Junior.

The waitress set the plates on the table. There were a few minutes of table quiet.

"Hey baby, can we get some more tea over here?" was heard over the café clatter.

Chief Maas, Byrd, and Twitty entered the Downtowner and sat at a nearby table.

Chief Maas stood and announced, "Listen up. We don't know much more than you do. No questions, please."

Kirkpatrick entered the restaurant, and the patrons all stood and applauded.

"Great tackle!" shouted Day Day.

Kirkpatrick waved them off and sat down with Chief Maas, Byrd, and Twitty.

Chapter 21

Jemilla Parks was led into Tee's cell. She brought him a Bible and some sports magazines. The Bible had a card inside with certain scriptures for Tee to read. She reminded him that they were waiting on the pending autopsy report, due in the next two days. She revealed to Tee that there might possibly be another suspect. She had Tee recall the last moments before he fired.

Tee stated that he was very nervous and was shaking before he fired.

Two witnesses had indicated they saw Tee leaving the window after the shot. They affirmed that the shot originated from his exact location. Three witnessed the reverend falling forward, as if forced from behind.

"That may be good news, but the case against you is mounting," said Jemilla.

Tee responded, "Good. Let's get on with it."

Before departing, Jemilla encouraged Tee to read the scriptures on the card she had placed in the Bible.

Tee seemed to be warming up toward Jemilla. She seemed at peace with herself, the same as Lillian from his childhood.

Chapter 22

The bus driver announced with much authority, "Listen up people! At our next stop you may disembark, grab a bite to eat, and use the restrooms. We will only be here for one hour. When you reboard, I will need to see your trip vouchers. You will find several fast-food restaurants at this stop. Remember, we will depart in one hour."

Annie Pearl disembarked and found a booth in the rear of the local diner. She watched the wall-mounted TV and heard the commentator announce that the investigation of Reverend Dalton's murder has been expanded. He concluded the fatal shot may have come from behind Dalton and not from the window of the building across the street, as many alleged.

Reboarding was no longer an option. Annie Pearl reached into her purse, grabbed her phone, and called her sister in Nashville, Tennessee. She told her sister that her vehicle had been stolen in Selma…could she please pick her up at the Pelham Diner in Pelham, Alabama. She did not tell her all the details, only that she was in a jam. Annie left the restaurant, found a dumpster behind the building, and tossed her pistol into it. She found a nearby trash can and discarded her purse.

76

Chapter 23

On a hunch, young Officer McCaleb went to the crime scene. He had been raised as an avid hunter. If Tee was shaking, as Tee had told his attorney, maybe he shot high and missed.

He surveyed the area and drew a line from the window of the building to where Dalton had stood before his execution. He traced the angle across the intersection to the old Woolworth's building. The wall was brick and mortar. He spent about two hours combing over the wall. Wow, there it was!

He looked closer, and the remains of the lead projectile were laying just below the spot on the sidewalk. The bullet had struck the brick wall on an edge where the brick and mortar were joined. The bullet left a sizable cavity and broken brick fragments. He collected the brick fragments and mangled bullet as evidence, brought them to the station, and reported to the chief.

Chief Maas was certain that Tee had missed, but he still needed more evidence against Ms. Jones.

"Good job, McCaleb. Now let's see if we can catch the real assassin."

"Yes sir."

Young Officer McCaleb was happy with his accomplishment. It would help vindicate Tee. McCaleb grabbed one of the police cameras, returned to the wall, and took numerous pictures. He tracked down Mrs. Parks and gave her the news of the find.

She immediately returned to the jail to give Tee the update.

"Well, Mr. Teital, someone is looking after you."

"Really?" replied Tee.

"We have mounting evidence that you missed Reverend Dalton."

Tee felt mixed emotions. Relief intermingled with indifference about Dalton's death. But he still wanted credit for the kill.

"Understand, Mr. Teitel, your charge will probably only be reduced to attempted murder, so don't start celebrating."

Chapter 24

Annie Pearl's sister arrived at the Pelham Diner just before dark. They went through a drive-thru to get some supper as they drove to Nashville. They arrived late and immediately went to bed. Annie Pearl was exhausted and slept hard.

She was awakened at about 9:30 A.M. with a loud knock. Her sister entered the room, sobbing.

"You didn't tell me everything about your trip. Your picture is all over the TV, every damn channel!" she screamed. "What happened?"

Annie Pearl yelled, "Dalton killed my boy, that's what happened! What would you do?"

When both women calmed down, Annie Pearl said, "I guess I should turn myself in."

Her sister agreed, "You can't run from this. Your hope is that you will receive leniency if Dalton is responsible."

"He is responsible!" she said and started crying again.

Annie Pearl called her neighbor, Etta, in Ohio. She had seen the news.

"Annie Pearl! You wouldn't believe the number of news vans and police cars around your house. I think they are going to kick in your front door and start looking for stuff."

Annie Pearl told her neighbor what had happened, including her son being hung.

"I don't blame you, but you can't run from them. I know it was probably worth it. I would have done the same thing," Etta admitted, her heart heavy for Annie Pearl, who had lost her only son in such a heinous and unforgivable murder.

Annie Pearl showered, borrowed clothing from her sister, and made herself look as presentable as possible. Her sister drove her to the police station in Nashville. She was read her rights, photographed, and placed into custody.

Chapter 25

The chief's secretary opened the door and said excitedly, "Chief, turn on your TV. Mrs. Jones just turned herself in at the Nashville police station."

"I know," said Maas. "I just got the call."

The chief's secure line buzzed.

"Yes?"

"Governor Wimple here. I suppose you have received the news?"

"Just got it," answered Maas.

"I know you're more relieved than I am," Governor Wimple said.

"Probably so," responded Chief Maas. "But there are many loose ends to tie up. We are far from over, but it's a start."

"How about we hold a press conference tomorrow in Selma?" said the governor.

"Okay, sounds good. Call me back with a time. I'll make the arrangements," replied Chief Maas.

When Jemilla Parks arrived at the jail, she found Tee reading the Bible. She looked upward and gave up a, "Thank You, Jesus!"

He looked up at her and said, "Thank you for this book, it seems to speak to me."

"That's the best news a man can have!" she said. She walked down the corridor and found Mr. Soda Pop staring at the ceiling.

"Sir, do you mind if I speak with you?"

"Are you some kind of detective?" he responded.

"No, I have a book to leave for you to read."

Soda Pop got to his feet and approached the Cell door. Jemilla handed him a Bible through the bars, along with a card of scriptures to read.

"So, you think this will help me?"

"I hope so," replied Jemilla. *I can only plant the seed*, she thought to herself.

Jemilla stopped by Tee's cell on the way out.

"Mr. Teitel?"

"Yes ma'am?"

"Would you allow me to pray with you?"

"Okay, I suppose," Tee replied.

Jemilla entered the cell as Big Ned watched through the bars.

"Almighty God, please reveal yourself to Mr. Teitel. Give him peace and a desire to have a relationship with you. Show him the wisdom of your Word, and your saving grace. In Jesus's name we pray, Amen."

Chapter 26

At 2:00 p.m. the following day, the press conference took place on the Dallas County Courthouse steps. Governor Wimple and Chief Maas were standing on the bottom step. Immediately behind them stood Officers Byrd, Twitty, Kirkpatrick, and McCaleb. On the third step stood Jemilla Parks and the state prosecutor.

Governor Wimple stepped forward to the microphone and gave a long-winded speech, hoping to gain some political points.

He concluded, "I have always been fair and supportive of the civil rights movement. Now, I will turn the press conference over to the man who designed the strategy to prevent Micah William's death, Chief Maas."

"Thank you, Governor Wimple," Chief Maas replied. Let me first, credit officers Byrd and Twitty for exposing the plot to murder Micah Williams and embedding themselves in the perpetrator's camp." Clearing his throat, he added, "These men are real heroes. In addition, Officer Kirkpatrick displayed courage well beyond the call of duty. He prevented the attempt on Micah

William's life and apprehended our suspect within a matter of minutes."

Buddy Dence was there. CNN, ABC, CBS, and NBC all were on hand. Cameras and microphones were everywhere.

Questions followed.

"Chief Maas, is it true that a second suspect has been arrested?"

"Yes, that suspect is being transported to Selma today. The suspect turned herself in to authorities yesterday. I think most of you have seen this on TV. I will remind you that the suspect is only a suspect and will be considered innocent until otherwise proven."

"Governor Wimple, do you believe that this senseless act has derailed your political aspirations?"

"Of course not, this situation has been handled in a most professional manner. Justice will be swift and certain," the governor replied.

"Chief, what about the person that shot from the window, where is he?"

"He is here in jail awaiting arraignment. Probably attempted murder charges. There is no evidence showing that he was the actual assassin."

"Chief, what about the two black men that were hung? Have they been identified? Do you have any suspects?"

Chief answered, "Well, no, is the answer to the first question. However, one of the victims may be connected to Reverend Dalton's murder. We can't say any more on that matter."

"Chief, what about the soldier that attempted to poison Micah Williams?"

Chief stated emphatically, "He was no soldier! I'm told by Colonel Hegedorn that the uniform he wore was stolen from the Nation Guard encampment. One more question."

"Was the attempt on Reverend Williams's life connected in some way to Reverend Dalton?" asked Buddy Dence.

"I can't comment on that at this time, no further questions for me. Due to the sensitive nature of evidence gathering, Officers Byrd and Twitty cannot answer questions."

"Miss Parks, who represents Mr. Teitel, would like to issue a statement. Go ahead, Miss Parks."

"My client will plead 'not guilty' at his arraignment tomorrow. There is no evidence showing that he is the assassin. My client is physically very sick. We would like to move forward, so he can enjoy his remaining days."

Chapter 27

THE NEXT DAY, AFTER TEE'S ARRAIGNMENT, THE STATE attorney said that he would reduce the charges against Tee to attempted murder. Further, if Miss Parks asked for a probated sentence, he would defer to the judge. Tee would then be charged with the illegal discharge of a firearm within the city limits. The attorney further stated that he was conferring with the judge momentarily.

Jemilla headed directly to the jail and informed Tee. He seemed to be happy that he would only be charged with attempted murder. Jemilla looked directly at Tee and said, "All blessings flow from God. Do you get it?"

Tee looked at Jemilla and said, "Thank you."

Jemilla's cell phone rang. She listened to the prosecutor, and her eyes welled with tears. She glanced over at Tee, who was now bewildered.

"Hallelujah, thank You, Jesus!" she shouted.

The prosecutor met with the judge, and he and the state attorney dropped the charge of attempted murder. Tee's only charge would be the illegal discharge of a firearm.

"If you will plead guilty to that charge, you will receive a $5,000 fine and community service for this probated sentence. Well, Mr. Teitel, what do you think?"

"I think I'm going home soon, right?" Tee replied.

"Yes, but not today. Maybe in a day or two. We shall see. I hope you realize that God had a hand in this," Jemilla replied.

"I think you are correct," said Tee.

Mr. Soda Pop, overhearing the conversation, stood up, grabbed the cell bars, and screamed, "You people are crazy! There is no God!"

Tee knew better and was now convinced that the wisdom in Jesus's teachings could only have originated from a higher power. He now knew there was a God, but he did not know God.

Jemilla gave Tee more scriptures to read, suggesting he might want to read the book of Matthew.

Chapter 28

ANNIE PEARL JONES ARRIVED IN SELMA AND WAS MET by a crowd of media and bystanders shouting questions and hateful obscenities. Two national news outlets were present, along with print media. Buddy Dence, now employed by a national newspaper from the D.C. area, was there to record the event.

Annie Pearl was escorted into the women's area of the jail, where she would await her arraignment.

Mr. Soda Pop was arraigned the following day. He entered a plea of not guilty to a charge of attempted murder and murder of the first degree for the poisoning of the two Cahaba victims. He stated he had no money and could not afford an attorney. The judge appointed him counsel, and a court date was set. He was denied bail. He later met with the court appointed attorney, and the two concluded they should try and strike a plea deal with the state attorney.

The weary Mr. Soda Pop said he had the names of his accomplices who were still at large. He pinned the assassination plan of Reverend Williams on the late Pal Dalton. He revealed the identity of the contact person who provided Dalton with the march security plans, claiming in confidence, fear of retribution if he were to unmask the identity of Von Doon. He stated there was likely considerable cash, at least $50,000, used to bribe the police officers, emphasizing that Dalton always had access to large amounts of cash from unknown sources. He had met the two Cahaba victims the day before their murders, as they were not part of Dalton's permanent security team. He suspected they had always been considered expendable. He was adamant Reverend Dalton had poisoned the two martyrs and had prepared the two deadly water bottles that Soda Pop tried to deliver to Reverend Williams.

Chapter 29

Ms. Annie Pearl Jones stood before the judge and entered a plea of "not guilty" to first degree murder.

Her sister had contacted an attorney friend of the family from Huntsville, who agreed to serve as Annie Pearl's attorney.

After consulting with her sister, the judge felt confident if Dalton and his thugs killed her son, she would receive a reduced charge and subsequent sentence. He concluded that nothing was certain, and a lot would depend upon the evidence recorded in Mr. Soda Pop's trial.

Chapter 30

Tee was jolted from his afternoon nap by Big Ned yelling, "Tee, Wake up! You have some visitors!"

Tee rolled off his metal slat bed and rubbed his sleepy eyes. Two figures standing in the doorway came slowly into focus, Jemilla Parks with the Reverend Micah Williams. Jemilla introduced Micah to Tee.

Tee responded, "I've seen you on TV several times."

"Jemilla tells me you've been reading your Bible. Is that right?" asked Micah.

"Yes," said Tee.

"May I pray with you?" said Reverend Williams.

"Yes sir," said Tee.

Jemilla put her hand on Tee's shoulder as Micah began the sinner's prayer.

He asked Tee to repeat after him, "Heavenly Father, we come before You in all sincerity, humble in spirit as I ask for You to forgive me. I have sinned and fallen short. I realize there is nothing I can do to earn my way to heaven. I believe You sent Your Son,

Jesus, to take on my sin. I ask for Your forgiveness, and I believe that Your only Begotten Son, Jesus, died for me. I believe He rose from the dead, and I believe I shall be with Him one day in my life after death. Thank you, God. In Jesus's name I pray. Amen, and Amen!"

Tee was now a child of God, born again; an heir of the Lord's. This became clear to Tee. Tears rolled down his cheeks. He looked at Jemilla and then hugged her.

"Please forgive me, Jemilla, I see you now as a sister in the Lord."

He saw Big Ned looking on through the now open door.

"Ned, please forgive me. I am so sorry for the things I said to you."

Big Ned said, "It's okay, my brother. You were lost. We all were at one time." Big Ned moved away from the now open door. "You are free to go, Mr. Teitel."

Tee checked out with the desk officer. He collected his keys, wallet, sunglasses, cigarettes, and change. He walked out of the building a free man. It felt good. He was a new person. He had the power over sin and the forgiveness of his Father in heaven. All things were new. He tossed the cigarettes in a nearby trash can.

Jemilla and Micah gave Tee a ride to his old Mercedes station wagon.

Jemilla looked at Tee and said, "Later this week, you need to pay your fine and schedule your community service."

"Tee?" Micah added.

"Yes sir?"

"Don't make being a Christian hard. You are no longer condemned by the law. The future sins you may commit will convict you and point you to the cross. Your sins hung on the cross with Jesus. When you do mess up, remember forgiveness is there for you, just ask for it and then repent. Find yourself a Bible-believing church and be involved."

Tee again thanked them and drove himself home. He stopped, emptied his overstuffed mailbox, and parked in the garage. He sifted through the mail, throwing away the junk. He spotted an envelope from UAB Medical Center in Birmingham. He opened it with anticipation of bad news.

Mr. Teitle, we have been trying to reach you by phone with no success. Your latest lab work reveals that your cancer is now in full remission. Please contact us at your earliest convenience.

Tee was overwhelmed with this miracle, and gave up his first, "Thank You, Jesus!" He called Jemilla with the news.

After another, "Thank You, Lord!" Jemilla said, "Tee, God has had His hand in this all along. You are experiencing what living by God's grace offers. Even if the news had been bad, death has no sting now. To be absent from the body is to be present with the Lord, and He will give you the grace to walk through whatever this life throws at you."

Chapter 31

CHIEF MAAS SUMMONED OFFICERS CAUSBY AND McCaleb to his office.

"I want you to drive north of town on the Summerfield Road and proceed to the Camp Grist area. I can't tell you where to go after that but explore every dirt road and path. Find Von Doon. Take all day if necessary. Be careful, he may be dangerous. He knows we are onto him. If possible, bring him in," said Chief.

The officers proceeded as instructed. After several unsuccessful hours of bad luck, they came to a dead end on a two-rut dirt road. From there was a path through dense woods, thickets, and vines. They followed on foot. Twenty minutes later, both patrolmen noticed an extremely foul smell. They continued deeper into the woods on the trail. Office Causby noticed buzzards circling overhead as they pressed on. The odor was thick. They came upon a very small clearing where they found a pit. It measured about 20 by 30 feet wide and six feet deep. They peered into the hole; McCaleb began to gag. The soupy pit was full of deer guts, feral pig parts, and three partially submerged bodies.

The buzzards and varmints had been feasting on the entrails, and their eyes were pecked out.

The officers placed tissues in their nostrils and this time approached from the upwind side. Causby snapped several pictures. The bloated bodies appeared to be of black men, their wrists cuffed to one another. The men were spooked by what they had seen. There was evil in the air.

Indeed, Von Doon was watching them from 40 yards away, concealed in the thicket.

They retraced their steps back to the squad car with pistols drawn. They radioed the chief they were inbound and described what they had found.

The officers arrived back at the station and said, "Chief, we must have walked two miles. It was awful."

Causby blurted, "There is no way to get equipment down this trail, it is just a path."

"The woods are too thick," said McCaleb.

"He is right, maybe a helicopter could drop a trash pump on location, and we could drain the pit," added Causby.

"I got it," said Chief Maas after studying the photos. The cuffs on the bodies were one clue; the area was another. Von Doon may have wanted to eliminate any forthcoming evidence from members of Dalton's entourage. Chief had Soda Pop transferred to Montgomery and placed in a maximum-security cell for his own protection. He could have no visitors.

The following day, Chief Maas obtained a helicopter from the National Guard. After a 45-minute search, they located the death pit about 15 miles north of town.

There was not enough open space to land the helicopter

safely. The helicopter hovered 50 feet above the hole. The down wash from the blades moved the slime around enough to see that the bodies were gone.

Chief and Causby observed from the helicopter. There was no visible trace, no visible tracks. The bodies were just not there.

Chief Maas had the pilot circle the surrounding forest, searching for any vehicles, structures, roads, any clues…

Nothing.

Upon their return, the Chief Maas conferred with Causby and Stallworth. They would make one more attempt at discovery—this time, with dogs. Surely, if the bodies had been drug away, they must have left scent that the dogs might be able to follow, the chief surmised.

The next morning, Officers Causby and Stallworth drove to the area with two dogs. Both animals had been trained for tracking wounded deer by blood trail and scent. The dogs pulled and tugged the officers down the path until they arrived at the clearing. They led the dogs around the pit.

The dogs got excited; one began to bark. They found a scent. They released the dogs and followed them as best they could through the woods, tripping and stumbling along the way. Two hundred yards later, they came upon a recently killed deer. They dogs were quite happy with themselves and did not want to leave the dead animal. The tattered officers continued to work the area, but the dogs always returned to the dead deer.

Back at the station, Chief Maas concluded Von Doon had killed the deer and had placed it there to hamper the search.

Gail knocked on the door and entered.

"Chief, I may have some more bad news for you."

Chief replied, "That's okay. Pile it on. I'm almost numb to it."

"Well, the files on Von Doon, including his application form, are missing."

Chief looked blankly into space. *Could it get any worse?* he thought.

"Thanks Gail." Von Doon was not just evil; he was also shrewd.

An hour later, Gail buzzed the chief.

"Sir, there are two gentlemen here that need some guidance, of sorts."

"Oh yeah?" answered Maas. "Send them in." There was something in Gail's voice that made Chief think this was going to be out of the ordinary.

The two older white men entered, their body odor preceded them into the room. Hygiene was not a priority with these two.

"Yes?" said Chief Maas as the two stood in front of his desk.

"We need to know how to collect the rest of our money."

Chief looked at them, raised his eyebrows and said, "Explain."

"Well, Reverend Dalton's people gave us each $100, and said we would get the other $100 after the march. The hotel said he ain't around here no more; he must have checked out of the hotel."

Chief replied sarcastically, "Oh, he's checked out, alright. As in permanently. You might need to make a claim on his estate, but we can't help you with that. By the way, what did you do to earn the money?"

"Uh, we dressed up in sheets and showed up at the bridge and sang Dixie," answered the one with the most teeth. The two disappointed men sauntered out of Chief Maas's office and passed Gail's desk, grumbling, leaving the door open.

Chief Maas yelled at Gail, "Girl, don't do that to me again!" He chuckled to himself.

"Chief, I thought you might need something to brighten your day! They were a hoot!"

"Yes, they were," said the chief.

Chapter 32

THE MONTHLY GATHERING OF THE OLD CHILDHOOD friends met up at the Tally Ho Lounge. The cigarette smoke lingered like a stratus cloud near the ceiling. Twitty, Byrd, Day Day, Jimbo, Randy, Junior, Nebro, and Maas were joined by Gail and some of the local girls from the same era. The quarters dropped into the jukebox.

Gail selected "What Does It Take?" by Junior Walker.

Jimbo chose "Honky Tonk Women" by the Stones.

Chief Maas yelled out, "Play 'Rainy Night in Georgia'!"

Byrd got up and danced with Gail, and when "Rainy Night in Georgia" played, Chief Maas pulled his wife onto the floor for a slow dance. Salads and steaks were served, and as they finished their dinner, a patron played "Wipeout" on the Jukebox. They sat in stunned silence as he gyrated and skittered solo around the dance floor. They paid their checks, and as they were leaving, Chief Maas spotted Micah Williams and Jemilla Parks having dinner in the main dining room.

Chief approached the table, and Reverend Williams stood and shook his hand.

"Are we still on for tomorrow?" questioned the chief.

"Looking forward to it," Micah answered.

"Me too!" said Jemilla.

"Okay, we will try and be there around 2:00 P.M. Does that give you guys enough time to get ready after services?"

"Shouldn't be a problem," the reverend answered. "And Chief, thank you for saving Otis and me."

"Just part of the job," said the chief.

Chapter 33

IT WAS A GLORIOUS SPRING DAY IN SELMA. THE AZALEAS were nearing full bloom, dogwood trees were showing off, too. The sky was without clouds.

Byrd stopped by Tee's house. Tee answered the doorbell.

Byrd said, "Tee, grab your shorts. I am going to launch the boat for a spring tune-up ride and could use a little help."

"Sure, come on in, I'll be ready in a few minutes." Tee found some old denim shorts and a t-shirt. Ten minutes later, they left his house. Under the bridge, at 1:45 P.M., the 13-foot Boston Whaler eased out from the ramp.

It was a perfect day to be on the river. The 40-horsepower mercury pushed the Whaler across the water at a good clip. Tee was enjoying being outside. He had never felt better. He pointed out a large gator sliding off the bank. Byrd nodded. Fifteen minutes later, they rounded the bend and came up on the huge sandbar.

Byrd felt shame, remembering that it was only a few days ago that he was at this spot for all the wrong reasons. He would ask for forgiveness today. They beached the boat, and Byrd said to Tee, "It runs good, don't you think?"

"Great," Tee replied.

Out of the trees, above the sand, appeared Twitty and Kirkpatrick, followed by Day Day, Junior, Randy, Jimbo, Causby, and several members of his newly found church. Otis, Jemilla, Big Ned, and the Reverend Micah Williams appeared behind them. They all gathered at the shoreline. Tee began to be choked up with emotion, his eyes welling with tears.

Reverend Williams approached Tee and said, "My brother, are you ready to be baptized?"

"Yes sir!" exclaimed Tee.

The reverend waded into the water and Tee followed. Micah looked Tee in the eyes and said, "Do you believe God sent His Son, Jesus, to take on your sins?"

"I do."

"Do you believe that He died on the cross for you and rose from the dead?"

"I do."

Micah turned and asked the flock to pray with him for Tee.

"I baptize you in the name of the Father, the Son, and the Holy Spirit." He held Tee by the shoulders, tilted him back, and submerged him under the water.

Tee emerged with a big grin. He hugged several of the group, sought out Jemilla, and thanked her for her part in this.

Reverend Williams asked if anyone else would like to be baptized. Byrd and Twitty came forward and rededicated their lives. The crowd clapped, and they all held hands to the sky as they sang "Amazing Grace."

Tee felt a tap on his shoulder. He turned, and there stood the love of his life, Julia.

Chapter 34

Four months have passed, bringing in the dog days of summer.

Mr. Soda Pop was convicted of attempted murder and possession of an illegal substance. He received a total sentence of 25 years, a light sentence because all other witnesses were deceased or missing and could not defend themselves or contradict Soda pop's testimony.

An older black man came forward and testified that two black men rented his truck. When they returned the truck a couple of hours later, they gave him extra money to clean up the intense smell of spilled gasoline in the back of the truck. He never knew or saw Mr. Soda Pop, which helped Soda Pop's defense of murder one charges.

Annie Pearl Jones was convicted of third-degree murder and illegal possession of a firearm. Because of Dalton's part in the hanging of her son, the judge gave her leniency and sentenced her to 10 years in prison. Parole would be possible in just three years.

The Reverend Micah Williams is back in Atlanta, very active with his now worldwide ministry. Thousands of souls have been saved through his evangelism. Thousands more are having seeds sown through his efforts.

Little Miami is crowded with water skiers, boaters, swimmers, and partiers.

Governor Wimple's re-election campaign is in full swing. The Selma debacle had little effect on his poll numbers, and he is expected to win the election.

Officer Kirkpatrick has been promoted to lieutenant and has his own office. He has received a commendation from Governor Wimple for outstanding service.

Jemilla Parks is running for mayor and has a favorable chance to win.

Big Ned is still the jailer, but he and Tee have started a prison ministry in Montgomery, where they frequently visit with Annie Pearl Jones.

Tee teaches tennis to underprivileged children in Selma as part of his community service. Chief Maas, Byrd, and Twitty met at the Tally Ho over a steak dinner to determine what to do with the confiscated money. They came to an agreement they would donate $200,000 cash anonymously to Micah William's ministry.

After paying for the steak dinners, the remaining money would be used to beef up the Selma Police Department with newer model squad cars and more officers hired.

The town of Selma remains pretty much the same, still struggling with hate, division, and unforgiveness. As the old song says, "Old times there are not forgotten."

Tee became consumed by the Bible. Many scriptures leapt off

the pages into Tee's heart. Jesus is real. There will be no turning back. Most of the television programs he now watches are pastors and teachers of the Word. He was particularly fond of Billy Graham and Micah Williams. He could now discern between the real men of God and the charlatans. Even when he was a lost soul, he knew Pal Dalton's message was a scam, 100 percent political and evil.

Tee and Julia found a small non-denominational church where the Word was more important than any doctrines. Love was more important than law. He would serve because he loved his Lord; he was an heir. He didn't serve to become an heir, he served because he was an heir to the Kingdom. He was so grateful the Holy Spirit had used Jemilla as a witness to him. He often looked back on his life and realized just how lost he was. He looks forward to the day he is united with his Lord and Savior… Maranatha!

Chapter 35

VON DOON REMAINS AT LARGE.

From the Author

The Voting Rights Act, signed into law on August 6, 1965, was a direct result of the famous Selma to Montgomery March. This act provided millions of black citizens the privilege to vote.

Unfortunately, the legislation could not heal the hearts of racists across this country. The root problems of hate and division can never be solved by legislation. Selma remains an example as of this writing in 2022. YES, progress has been made, but it has become a slow process. Both sides share the blame.

Selma has lost over 30 percent of its population. The town is considered by numerous surveys to be one of the worst places to live and raise a family in the U.S. Violent crimes in Selma are 60 percent above the national average.

Selma's local government struggles with corruption, violent crime, drugs, and filth. Selma is a dangerous place. Current leadership is inept or incapable and seems content with the status quo.

Martin Luther King realized that hate and violence can never be a cure or a substitute for transformation of hearts. The author strongly believes the only true solution is a relationship with Jesus.

As I stated earlier, this is a work of fiction. Tee's character is loosely based on a story revealed to the author. All other active characters are purely fictional. Any conclusions drawn as to whom certain characters resemble is left to you, the reader. No comparisons are intentional.

Sincerely,

Timothy E. Paul

These are some of Tee's
favorite Scriptures:

EPHESIANS 6:1-21
CORINTHIANS 1:18
ROMANS 12:1-2
JOHN 16:33
MATTHEW 9:13

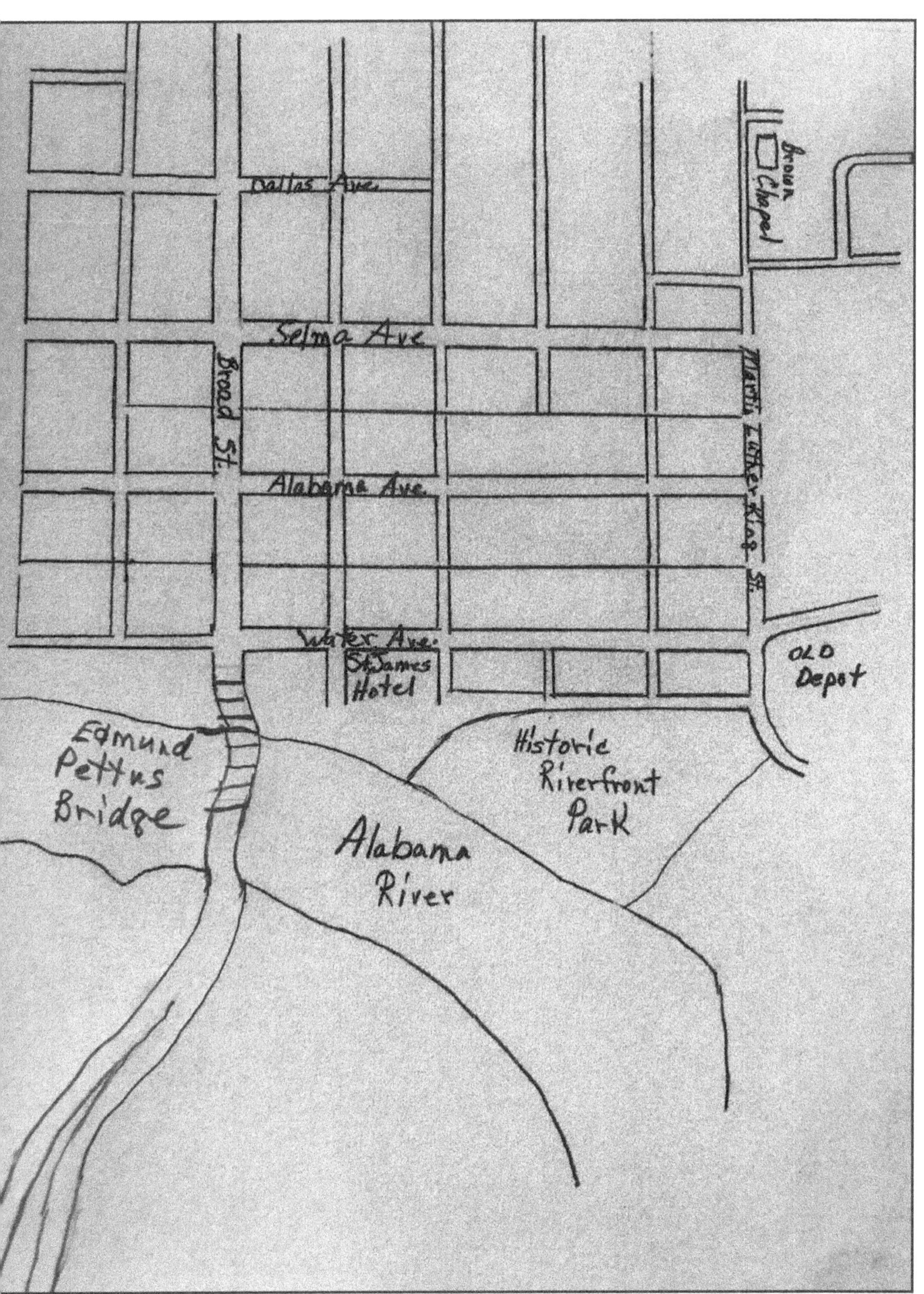

Brown Chapel
Dallas Ave.
Selma Ave.
Broad St.
Alabama Ave.
Martin Luther King St.
Water Ave.
St. James Hotel
OLD Depot
Edmund Pettus Bridge
Historic Riverfront Park
Alabama River